Bats, Bats, Bats

Written by Christine Price

STECK-VAUGHN
ELEMENTARY · SECONDARY · ADULT · LIBRARY

A Harcourt Classroom Education Company

www.steck-vaughn.com

Bats come out at night.

Bats live in groups.

Bats sleep upside-down.

Bats eat lots of bugs.

 5

Bats use sound to fly.

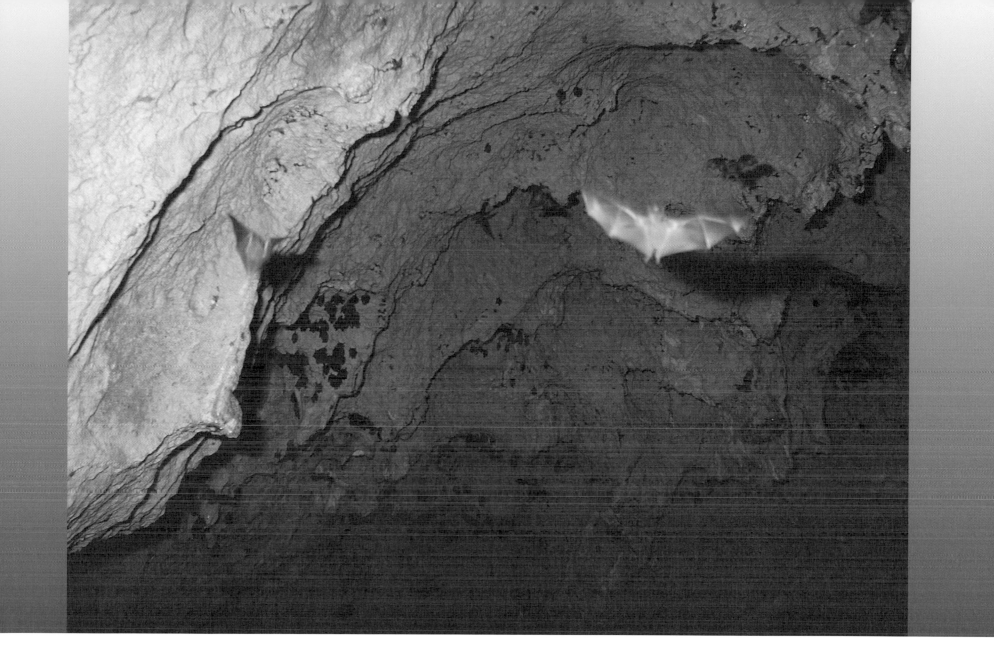

Bats live in caves.

Some bats live in bat houses.